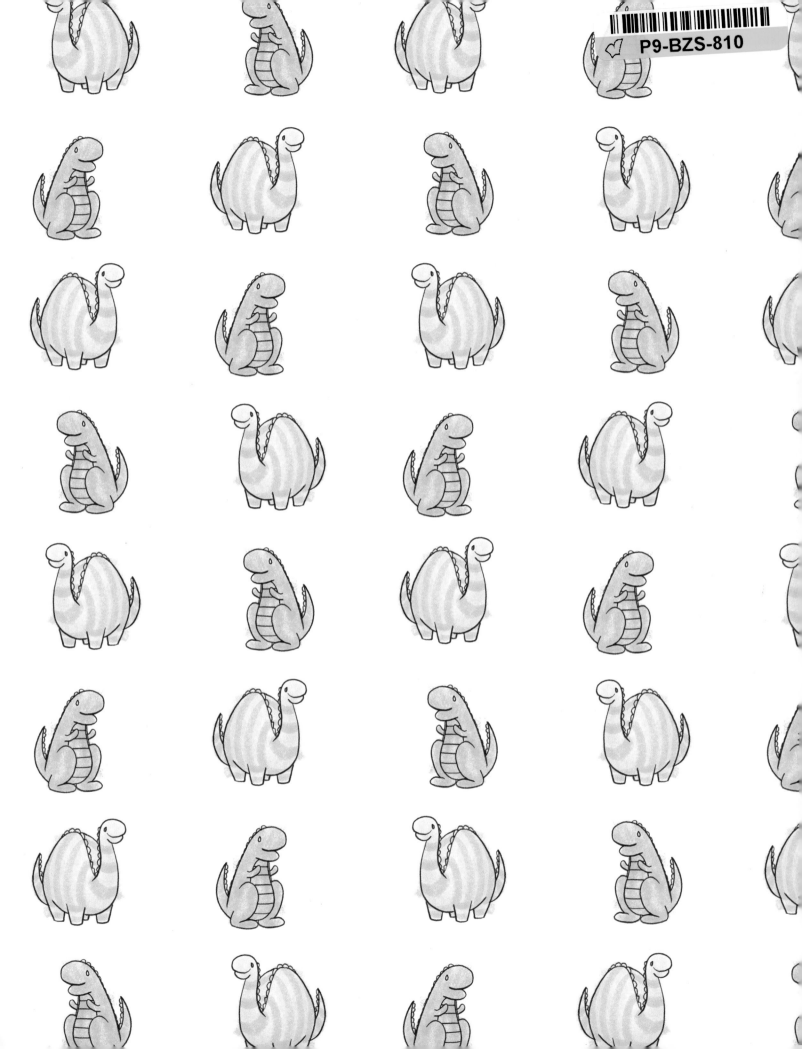

"The things that make me different are the things that make me ME."
— (Piglet), A.A. Milne, *Winnie-the-Pooh*

To my agent and friend, Ronnie Ann Herman.
Thank you for believing in me. — R.T.

STERLING CHILDREN'S BOOKS
New York

An Imprint of Sterling Publishing Co., Inc.
1166 Avenue of the Americas
New York, NY 10036

ISBN 978-1-4549-2123-3

Distributed in Canada by Sterling Publishing Co., Inc.
c/o Canadian Manda Group, 664 Annette Street
Toronto, Ontario, Canada M6S 2C8
Distributed in the United Kingdom by GMC Distribution Services
Castle Place, 166 High Street, Lewes, East Sussex, England BN7 1XU
Distributed in Australia by NewSouth Books
45 Beach Street, Coogee, NSW 2034, Australia

For information about custom editions, special sales, and premium and corporate purchases, please contact Sterling Special Sales at 800-805-5489 or specialsales@sterlingpublishing.com.

Manufactured in China

Lot #:
2 4 6 8 10 9 7 5 3 1
05/17

www.sterlingpublishing.com

The illustrations were created using oil-based pencils, watercolor, and digital media.

Design by Heather Kelly

ALLY-SAURUS
& the Very Bossy Monster

by Richard Torrey

STERLING CHILDREN'S BOOKS
New York

"Hold still, Ally," said Mother.

"My name is not Ally, it's Ally-saurus!" said Ally-saurus.

"Very well, ALLY-SAURUS," said Mother.

"Hold still while I fix your hair."

"Dinosaurs don't fix their hair," said Ally-saurus.

"They do if they want to go outside and play," said Mother.

"**ROAR!**" said Ally-saurus.

Dressed in her favorite dinosaur shirt, Ally-saurus chomped her cinnamon toast with fierce teeth.

"It looks like a dinosaur," said Ally-saurus.

"We don't play with our food," said Father.

" ROAR! " said Ally-saurus.

After breakfast, Ally-saurus roared and stomped through the jungle.

Her friend, Kai, danced across a grand stage.

And Kai's brother, Petey, ran around shouting," BEAR! "

All morning they stomped, roared, danced, and laughed.

Then Maddie showed up.

"STOP!"

Ever since Maddie moved next door, things had been different.

"Everyone has to get in line behind me—that's the rule!"

"If the ball bounces twice and hits a flower, I win. That's the rule!"

"You have to catch the next grape in your mouth, or I get all of your grapes. That's the rule!"

Yes, Maddie was *always* making up rules.

"You have to . . . you can't . . . you mustn't . . . you must . . . if you won't . . . if you can't . . . if you don't . . . if you do . . ."

"Today we're going to play monsters," declared Maddie.

"And *I* get to be the queen monster because it was *my* idea. That's the rule."

"Fine," said Ally-saurus.

"I'll be a monster—a monster who's really a dinosaur. ROAR! "

"And I'll be a super, amazing, dancing monster," said Kai.

"And I'm inviting everyone to my super, amazing monster dance. TA-DA! "

"**BEAR!**" said Petey.

"**STOP!**" said Maddie.

"If you're going to play monsters, you have to follow the rules!"

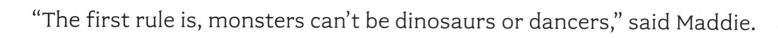

"The first rule is, monsters can't be dinosaurs or dancers," said Maddie.

"Monsters have to be hairy and ugly, with warts and horns."

"*Hairy and ugly?*" said Ally-saurus.

"*Warts and horns?*" said Kai.

"That's the rule!" said Maddie.

"*Bear!*" said Petey.

"Monsters can't say 'Roar' or 'Ta-Da!' either," said Maddie.

"Monsters can only say scary things like 'GRACK-A-CRACK!'"

"I don't want to say 'Grack-a-crack,'" said Ally-saurus.

"I don't even know how," said Kai.

"Bear!" said Petey.

"And monsters *never* go to super, amazing monster dances," said Maddie.

"Monsters only do scary and smelly and slimy things!"

"*Smelly and slimy?*" said Ally-saurus.

"*Yuck and double-yuck!*" said Kai.

"That's the rule!" said Maddie.

"*Bear!*" said Petey.

"And finally, monsters *never* carry teddy bears," insisted Maddie.

"***That's*** the rule!"

"ROARRRRRRRRRRR!" said Ally-saurus.

"If **you** are going to play monsters with **us**," she said, "**you** have to follow the rules!"

"The first rule is: we can be any kind of monster we want to be," said Ally-saurus. "Hairy and ugly, a dancer . . . even a dinosaur!"

"We can say whatever we want to say:
'Grack-a-crack,' 'Roar!,' or 'Ta-Da!'

And if we want to, we can go to a super,
amazing monster dance!"

"And finally," said Ally-saurus, "**nobody** takes Petey's teddy bear! **That's** the rule!"

And with that, Ally-saurus, Kai, and Petey got all dressed up
and went to the super, amazing monster dance . . .

. . . where they stomped, roared, danced, and laughed all afternoon.

TA-DA!

ROAR!

Then Maddie showed up (*again*) . . .

. . . and joined the fun.

The next day, when Maddie said, "Everyone has to get in line behind me—that's the rule!" . . .

. . . Ally-saurus said, " ROAR! "

And they stomped, roared, danced, and laughed all the way to school.

GRACK-A-CRACK!